¡VAMOS!
Let's Go Read

by Raúl the Third
colors by Elaine Bay

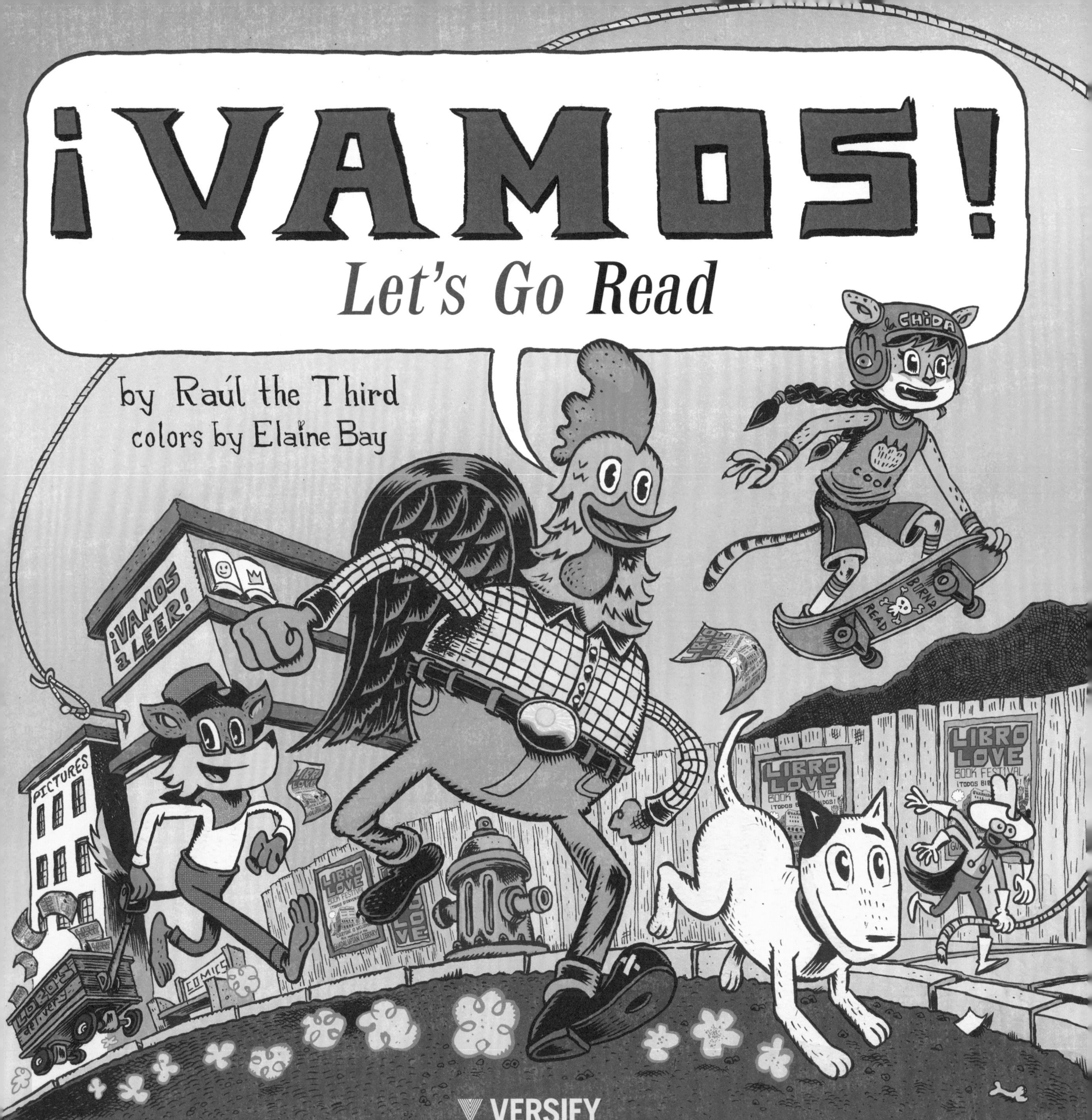

VERSIFY
An Imprint of HarperCollins*Publishers*

To grocery store paperbacks, comic book spinner racks at the 7-Eleven, paper bag book covers that I filled with doodles, used bookstores, and without a question, to the librarians who encouraged a boy to read and draw— especially my favorite librarian, Cathy Camper, who made all of this possible!
—Raúl

To the people who help make books accessible to all.
—Elaine

Versify® is an imprint of HarperCollins Publishers.

¡Vamos! Let's Go Read
Copyright © 2023 by Raúl Gonzalez III
¡Vamos! is a registered trademark of Raúl Gonzalez.
All rights reserved. Manufactured in Italy. No part of this book may be used or reproduced
in any manner whatsoever without written permission except in the case of brief quotations
embodied in critical articles and reviews. For information address HarperCollins Children's Books,
a division of HarperCollins Publishers, 195 Broadway, New York, NY 10007.
www.harpercollinschildrens.com

Library of Congress Control Number: 2023930165
ISBN 978-0-35-853936-0

The artists used pen and ink on smooth plate Bristol board to create the illustrations for this book.
Colors were created with Adobe Photoshop.
Flatting by Julie Lerche
Hand lettering by Raúl Gonzalez III
Design by Whitney Leader-Picone
23 24 25 26 27   RTLO   10 9 8 7 6 5 4 3 2 1

First Edition

Little Lobo and his friends have spent all morning hanging up a special invitation all around town.

Every year the library celebrates books and their community with an out-of-this-world book festival! Everyone in town looks forward to the big event!

The Guadalupian Library was built when the desert town was under the ocean. Books written by trilobytes, ancient sea creatures, are the oldest in the collection.

calamar

medusa

tiburón

estrella del mar

The library has always welcomed change and all of the creatures who have wandered or swam through its doors.

Little Lobo and his friends each love the library for different reasons.

Little Lobo traces out new routes for his deliveries in the map room.

I know these cities like the back of my paw!

Bernabé likes to read romance novels in the tea room.

Kooky Dooky loves to play video games while listening to books on tape in the computer room.

Coco Rocho reads countless books about legendary vaqueros.

La Chida borrows tools and manuals that teach her how to build ramps for her skatepark.

They're all looking for a special book. Little Lobo is missing issue four of *Lucha Comix*. Bernabé hopes to find the *Puppy Love* Valentine's Day special.

monedas

Coco Rocho is searching for *Secret Graffiti Language of the Cowboy Cucarachas*.

Kooky Dooky is looking for *Gallos of the Corn* to complete his Estefan Rey collection.

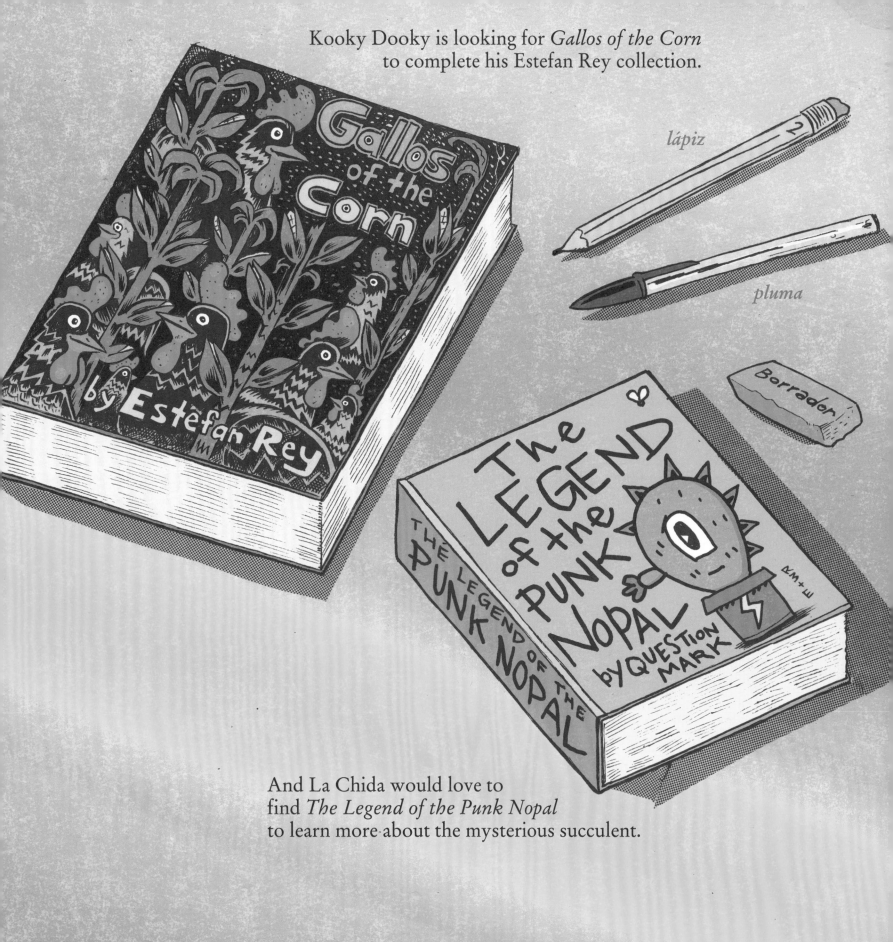

And La Chida would love to find *The Legend of the Punk Nopal* to learn more about the mysterious succulent.

Señorita Páginas and her team of bibliotecarias organized the festival. . . .

They worked day and night to make it a celebration of books and the community they serve.

The festival takes place both in the library and around it.

There is so much to see . . .

disfraces

Long lines lead to the festival's special guests.

Ricky Ratón signs copies of his autobiography, *Only Ricky: My Life in the Ring before El Toro.*

Is El Toro here?

RICKY RATÓN

Editor's Note: Wait—if Ricky's here, whose statue is in the park? (¡Vamos! Let's Cross the Bridge, p. 25)

Cameras flash, and fans take selfies with Grumpy Burro, who is an internet sensation.

autofoto

click!
click

grumpy burro

$1 per selfie

NOT 4 SALE

DON'T FEED ME CARROTS! BUY MY CALENDAR! $5.00 SIGNED $10.00

Burro Joe and Pato Peeko make recipes from their latest cookbook.

La Oink Oink teaches wrestling fans how to design luchadores based on themselves.

Puppetro carves puppets of all the children visiting the festival.

Mr. Posada prints the comics made in Señor Duende's workshop.

fotocopiadora

His students organize and fold their pages.

Using his book stapler, Mr. Posada puts the comic book pages together.

THUNK!

grapadora

You are all authors now. Share your stories with the world.

People come to the library for many different reasons. Señora González found a place for her li'l burritos to focus their energy, take English classes while they read, and eat snacks provided by the library.

Don Ruffino studied to become a permanent resident of La Frontera at classes held in the library.

He sculpted the statue in the courtyard as a thank-you.

estatua

At the festival, there are many vendors who have set up booths, each specializing in something different.

As they walk, Little Lobo finds his issue of *Lucha Comix* at Bill's Coins, Cards, Stamps, and Comics.

La Chida and Coco Rocho find their books at the Time Capsule.

And finally, the librarians bring them to their masterpiece: the Ride into Books.

There are so many to choose from!

GLOSSARY*

*These are only some of the words found in Little Lobo's story. Be sure to look up other ones you don't know in a Spanish-English dictionary!

(El) **Amor** – Love
(La) **Autofoto** – Selfie
(La) **Biblioteca** – Library
(Las) **Bibliotecarias** – Librarians
Bienvenidos – Welcome
(El) **Borrador** – Eraser
(La) **Brocha** – Brush
(El) **Búho** – Owl
(El) **Burro** – Donkey
(El) **Calamar** – Squid
(El) **Cantor** – Singer
(El) **Casco** – Helmet
Chida – Cool
(Los) **Cocineros** – Cooks
(El) **Conocimiento** – Knowledge
(La) **Cucaracha** – Cockroach
(El) **Cuchillo** – Knife
(Los) **Deportes** – Sports
(El) **Dibujo** – Drawing
(Los) **Disfraces** – Costumes
(El) **Elote** – Grilled corn on the cob

(El) **Escalofrío** – Shiver
(El) **Estante para libros** – Bookshelf
(La) **Estatua** – Statue
(La) **Estrella del mar** – Starfish
(La) **Fotocopiadora** – Copy machine
(La) **Frontera** – Border
(El) **Gallo** – Rooster
(El) **Gato** – Cat
(Los) **Globos** – Balloons
(La) **Grapadora** – Stapler
Hechos en casa – Homemade
(Los) **Hijos** – Children
(El) **Hombre** – Man
(El) **Lápiz** – Pencil
(La) **Leche tibia** – Warm milk
Leer – To read
(El) **Libro** – Book
(El) **Lobo** – Wolf
(La) **Lucha** – Struggle
(El) **Luchador** – Wrestler
(El) **Maíz** – Corn

(Las) **Manos** – Hands
(La) **Manzana** – Apple
(La) **Máscara** – Mask
(La) **Medusa** – Jellyfish
(Las) **Monedas** – Coins
(La) **Mosca** – Fly
(El) **Nopal** – Prickly pear cactus
(Las) **Páginas** – Pages
(La) **Patineta** – Skateboard
(El) **Pato** – Duck
(La) **Pluma** – Pen
Poder – To be able to, can
(El) **Pulpo** – Octopus
(El) **Ratón** – Mouse
(Los) **Sapos** – Toads
(El) **Taburete** – Stepstool
(El) **Tiburón** – Shark
Todos – All
(El) **Toro** – Bull
(La) **Tortuga** – Turtle
(El) **Vaquero** – Cowboy
(El) **Venado** – Deer

A NOTE FROM RAÚL THE THIRD

EVER SINCE the fateful day that my mom decided to take us to the library because she was sick and tired of our shenanigans in our tiny one-bedroom apartment, I have been obsessed with books and illustration. The library became a second home for us when we were kids.

I read so many books at our tiny library just off Festival Street that every summer I was given Certificates of Participation from the Texas State Library. But that's not all we did there. My mom took English classes and studied American history for her citizenship test. My two brothers and I participated in all kinds of cool activities from puppet making to my personal favorite: drawing!

One summer, a librarian suggested that I draw my favorite part of a book after I couldn't tell her what it was. From that point on, I started to pay close attention to the images that formed in my mind whenever I read a book, and my long journey to becoming an illustrator began. I copied so many drawings from all of my favorite illustrators that they called me "the human copy machine"!

If you look closely at the walls of the library in downtown El Paso, TX, you'll notice that they are covered in fossils dating back fifty million years, from when my hometown was at the bottom of the ocean. Every sentence and drawn line is like a fossil in that it contains the history of what inspired it. The creation of this book was thanks to the generosity and knowledge that a library shares with its patrons no matter where they are from or how much money they have. I will forever be grateful for my experiences there and for the amazing journey they inspired me to take.